Daniel Visits the Library

adapted by Maggie Testa

based on the screenplay "Calm for Storytime"

written by Wendy Harris

poses and layouts by Jason Fruchter

Ready-to-Read

Simoː
New York London Tː

SIMON SPOTLIGHT
An imprint of Simon & Schuster Children's Publishing Division
1230 Avenue of the Americas, New York, New York 10020
This Simon Spotlight edition August 2015
© 2015 The Fred Rogers Company
SIMON SPOTLIGHT, READY-TO-READ, and colophon are registered trademarks of Simon & Schuster, Inc.
For information about special discounts for bulk purchases, please contact Simon & Schuster Special Sales at
1-866-506-1949 or business@simonandschuster.com.
Manufactured in the United States of America 0120 LAK
6 8 10 9 7 5
ISBN 978-1-4814-4174-2 (eBook)
ISBN 978-1-4814-9683-4 (prop)

At last it is storytime!

"Ribbit, ribbit," he says.

"I feel calmer," says Prince Wednesday.

We listen to the story.

X the Owl finishes the story.

"The end," he says.

Storytime is over.
Now we can go
outside and play.